S
Before you t
Take a piece of paper.
Pick up your pencil.
Draw a big triangle.

At the top point of the triangle write **Secret Government UFO Test Base**. At the left point write **Dinosaur Graveyard**. At the right point, **Humongous Horror Movie Studios**. And in the exact center of the triangle write, **Grover's Mill**.

Ah, Grover's Mill. A perfectly normal town, bustling with shops, gas stations, motels, restaurants, and schools. A small town with a great big heart, nestled snugly in the midst of —

Wait! Did we say *normal*? A studio where they film the cheapest horror movies ever made? The world's largest and smelliest graveyard of ancient dinosaur bones? A secret army base filled with captured alien spacecraft?

All this makes poor Grover's Mill the exact center of supreme intergalactic weirdness!

Turn the page.
If you dare.
Enter The Weird Zone!

There are more books about

THE WEIRD ZONE

THE WEIRD ZONE

GIGANTOPUS FROM PLANET X!

by Tony Abbott

Cover illustration by Broeck Steadman
Illustrated by Lori Savastano

SCHOLASTIC INC.

New York   Toronto   London   Auckland   Sydney
Mexico City   New Delhi   Hong Kong

For all the great folks at
The Dinosaur's Paw

Text copyright © 1997 by Robert Abbott.
Illustrations copyright © 1997 by Scholastic Inc.
All rights reserved. Published by Scholastic Inc.
SCHOLASTIC, THE WEIRD ZONE, and associated logos and designs are trademarks and/or registered trademarks of Scholastic Inc.

Printed in the U.S.A.

ISBN 0-439-22368-7

2 3 4 5 6 7 8 9 10   40   08 07 06 05 04 03 02

Contents

GIGANTOPUS FROM PLANET X!

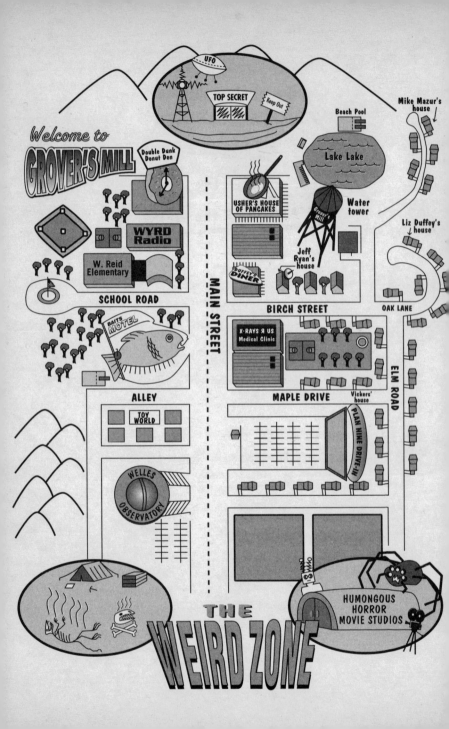

The morning air was warming up as Holly Vickers biked down Main Street in Grover's Mill.

"It's going to be hot today," said her best friend Liz Duffey, pedaling beside her.

"And weird, too," added Holly. "I have a feeling." Riding just ahead was her brother Sean and their friends Jeff Ryan and Mike Mazur.

Bong! came a loud gonging sound. The extra large donut clock on top of the Double Dunk Donut Den was chiming the morning hour.

Sssss! The oversized pancake pan on the

roof of Usher's House of Pancakes hissed even louder.

On their right they passed W. Reid Elementary School and the big fish-shaped Baits Motel. Across the street stood the X-rays Я Us Medical Clinic.

Liz turned to Holly as they rode along. "Everything seems pretty normal."

Holly nodded at Liz. It did feel normal. It felt normal because everything was so weird. That's because weird *is* normal in Grover's Mill.

Grover's Mill. A place she and her friends call . . . The Zone. The Weird Zone. A place where really normal things never happen. Ever.

And Holly and her friends were on their way to one of the weirdest places in The Zone. Humongous Horror Movie Studios. Everything there was a creepy set, an icky prop, or a cheesy costume for cheap, sometimes scary, always not-so-good horror movies.

"Wow!" gasped Mike, stopping with

everyone else at the end of Main Street. "There it is!"

An old airplane hangar just outside of town was home to Humongous Studios. It looked like a huge soup can cut in half and laid on its side. It even had ridges across the curved roof.

"It's . . . it's . . . humongous!" Jeff sputtered.

"That's the idea," said Sean. "Dad needed a big place to make big movies!"

Holly and Sean's father, Todd Vickers, owned Humongous Studios. But he was the only one who worked there. He wrote, directed, produced, acted in, filmed, and built the props for every Humongous horror movie.

Today, Mr. Vickers was filming a new movie. And he was going to show the kids how he made movie magic.

A few minutes later, the five friends parked their bikes outside the huge hangar.

"Enter, if you dare," said Sean, grinning.

Eeeee-oooo-eeee! **Creepy organ music floated all around the kids as they stepped inside.**

"With horror movies," said Sean, "you gotta have creepy music. It comes with the territory."

The five kids stepped into a vast room. Out in the middle of the floor was a large lumpy shape covered with a black canvas cloth.

"Ah," said Sean, with a little smile. "Maybe a new prop. Let's take a peek."

"I wouldn't do that," said Holly.

Sean shrugged and moved in front of Holly. He started to pull the cloth off but at the last minute he pushed Holly ahead of him.

"Aaaaaah!" she shrieked as two huge spiked claws whipped out from under the cloth and closed tightly around her!

"Hey!" cried Jeff. "A giant claw thing is eating Holly!"

As Holly struggled to free herself from the gnarly claws, she noticed that the crea-

4

ture's hard shell was flaking apart in her hands. And it smelled like fresh paint.

"Wait a second!" she said. "Dad, are you in there?" She tried to see under the cloth. "Dad? Okay, put me down! Come on, Dad!"

ERKKK! The claws stopped clawing, and Holly heard chuckling from inside the creature.

A moment later, the jaws opened and out popped the head of Todd Vickers. He had a camera on his shoulder and was beaming with delight. "Great scream, dear! Got it all on film!"

"Thanks a lot, Dad," mumbled Holly, slipping out from the claws and dusting the flaky bits of shell off her T-shirt.

"Welcome to another Humongous scream fest!" Mr. Vickers said cheerily. He whipped off the cloth to show a giant crab monster with two huge spiked claws and eyes on stalks. "I call him — *Clawgantua, the Clawed Avenger!* Poor Clawgantua. A freak aquarium mishap turns a tiny orphan named Crabcake into — "

"A giant crab with enormous claws called Clawgantua?" said Holly.

Mr. Vickers looked stunned. "There's just no keeping anything from you super-smart kids!"

Holly smiled back at her father. She loved him a lot, but the truth was Humongous movies were sort of, well, not so good. Props didn't work. Sets tumbled down. Makeup fell off. But the camera kept rolling.

"The camera must keep rolling," Mr. Vickers said. "You never know what might happen."

As the five kids followed Mr. Vickers around the hangar, they could see the whole strange movie studio.

In one corner was a jungle with a volcano. Next to that was a castle dungeon with painted stone walls and lots of chains. Behind that was a giant kitchen with huge forks and spoons and a pair of enormous scissors sitting on a tall table.

"A total horror playground!" said Mike.

"And look! The moon!" Mike stepped onto a bumpy landscape of crusty cardboard craters.

Mr. Vickers chuckled. "Actually, it's supposed to be Mars. But only astronauts would know the difference!"

"Or aliens," mumbled Liz.

Then the moviemaker said, "Behold, the den of mystery! The prop workshop!" He led them into a long room filled with worktables.

"Excellent!" gasped Sean. "Hairy hands. Zombie eyeballs. Rubber brains. This is where I'm coming for school supplies! Hey, what's this?" He pointed to a large black box on the floor.

"Careful with that, son," said Mr. Vickers. "That's a fog machine. One false move and we'll be in fog as thick as a vampire's accent!"

"This stuff is cool," said Jeff, slapping a fake scar on his cheek.

The director nodded. "Props, costumes, and makeup are the heart of a good story.

They transform normal folks into weird monsters."

Liz turned to Holly. "In The Zone, it's hard to tell the difference sometimes."

Just then — *Scritch!* Holly heard something moving outside the door.

"And you know, kids," said Mr. Vickers. "Movie stars come in all shapes and sizes, too. It just happens that I got a call this morning, and one of my . . . ah . . . *actors*, should be here very soon!"

"Cool!" said Jeff. "Can we meet him?"

Scritch! Holly moved closer to the door. She heard something for sure. "Dad, what's out — "

Suddenly, the door swung open and a long, green arm curled in and wrapped itself tightly around Holly's neck!

"Another thing is eating Holly!" cried Sean.

"Kkkkk!" she gagged as the long green arm yanked her out the door!

A Grabby Sort of Guy!

"**A** giant, real-live octopus!" screamed Mike.

That was the second-to-last thing Holly heard before things started to go dark. The last thing was her own voice, shrieking for help.

"Help-p-p-p!" she sputtered as she felt herself getting dragged across the ground.

Zzzzt! An electrical buzz sounded, and the green arm instantly uncoiled from Holly's neck and dropped to the ground with a thud.

"Wow! It's a giant octopus!" shouted Jeff. "Will you look at those tentacles!"

Holly looked up at the thing that had

grabbed her. "An octopus?" she gargled.

Yes! An octopus! And boy was it a big one! It had a giant speckled green dome and eight leathery tentacles wrapped like snakes around it. Two deep eyes glared out from the towering dome.

Sean frowned when he saw the creature was sitting on the back of a truck. "Oh, so, it's *not* a real octopus?"

"Now there's a movie star!" said Mr. Vickers, rubbing his hands together as he approached the truck. "I hope my new prop didn't scare you, Holly, dear!"

"No . . ." Holly rubbed her neck. "If not being able to breathe, watching your life flash before your eyes, and seeing a big bright light didn't scare me . . ."

Mr. Vickers smiled at her. "That's the spirit!"

Holly gulped. "Another second without air and I really *would* have been a spirit." She got to her feet and read the words painted on the truck's door. *Acme Beast and Creature Delivery.*

Next to the truck were two men in workmen's overalls. One held a clipboard and chewed on a pencil. The other, a chubby man, leaned against the back of the truck.

While Mr. Vickers went over to examine the octopus, the man with the clipboard stepped forward. "I'm delivering one . . ." He read his clipboard. "Slither-Matic Deluxe Octo-Prop."

"Eight legs!" blurted his chubby partner, still leaning against the truck. "It gives a hug like grandma and you need four humans just to shake hands with it! Ha!"

"Humans?" said Holly to herself. "I wonder why he said that . . ."

"Hey, missy, you gonna sign?" The man tapped his clipboard in Holly's face.

Holly pulled back. "Uh, sorry, I don't have anything to write with."

"Here ya go." The man yanked the pencil from his teeth and offered it to Holly.

Splat. Something green and slimy dripped off the end of the pencil. "Gum," the man said.

The other Acme man, who was still leaning against the back of the truck, began to laugh. His wide stomach shook like a bowlful of jellyfish. "Gum!" he snorted. "Dat's a good one!"

Holly swallowed hard and signed.

Suddenly, a soft voice spoke from the front of the truck. "Boys, help me down, won't you?"

Everyone turned to see the passenger door of the truck open and a leg slide out. A leg with a boot on it. A high, black boot.

The two delivery men hustled over.

A moment later, a woman stood next to the truck. She was tall, with lots of wavy red hair, bright red lipstick, and a green suit.

"Gosh!" murmured Jeff.

Sean nodded. "She smells like the perfume counter at Mallwarts!"

Mike nodded. "Lady, are you an actress?"

"AWWWK!" the woman exploded, nearly spitting. She covered her mouth and gig-

gled politely. "Er, no, not an . . . actress! He-he!"

Then the woman's expression changed. She stared at Holly. Really, she stared at Holly's shoulder. She stepped closer. "Is that a piece of . . . *crab shell* . . . on your shoulder?"

"Huh?" Holly looked at her shoulder. "Oh, no, this is from Clawgantua, the Clawed Avenger."

The woman eyed Holly's shoulder. Then she said, "I'd like to meet this Clawed Avenger."

"He's one of my dad's movie props," Holly said.

"Oh," said the woman. She seemed disappointed. "Never mind, then." She looked around and smiled sweetly at everyone. "I am Mary Smith! I will show you how to control your excellent new Slither-Matic Deluxe Octo-Prop. Here is the remote control unit."

She took a black box from a little pouch on her belt. "These eight buttons control the eight tentacles, and this red one stops the prop."

Mike and Jeff helped Mr. Vickers and the Acme men slide the giant octopus to the ground.

The woman named Mary Smith then gave Mr. Vickers the box. "If you run into any problems, I'll be staying at the lake." She pointed to the north end of Grover's Mill.

"Lake Lake?" said Liz. "But there's no place to stay at Lake Lake."

"You should stay at the Baits Motel," said Jeff. "It's really neat. It's shaped like a fish."

"A fish!" The woman smacked her lips. "Mmm!" Then she turned to the delivery men. "Take me to the fish place, will you, boys?"

"Aye-aye, Miss Jones," said the man with the clipboard. "Me and my partner would love to!"

Holly's eyebrows went up. "Excuse me," she said to the woman with red hair. "But

I thought you said your name was Mary *Smith*."

The woman turned and looked deep into Holly's eyes. "Did I?" Then without another word, she climbed into the truck, and it roared off toward Grover's Mill, leaving a cloud of dust behind it.

"Did anybody notice how totally weird that was?" asked Holly.

"Weird?" said Liz. "Compared to what?" She picked another bit of crab shell from Holly's shirt.

Mike bent to sniff the Octo-Prop. Sean and Jeff poked its leathery skin and smiled.

Holly rolled her eyes. "Never mind."

"I shall name you — Gigantopus!" Mr. Vickers said with glee to the Octo-Prop. "Warm up those tentacles, because I'm going to make you a star!"

The enormous octopus prop sat spread out on the sandy ground. The dome was large enough to fit a whole house inside it. Each of the octopus's eight long tentacles stretched thirty feet out from the center.

"He sure is a big guy!" said Mike, gently touching the rubbery green skin. He sniffed it again. "He smells like my mom's fish sticks!"

Mr. Vickers's eyes beamed with excitement as he lifted the camera to his shoulder. "We start filming immediately. Watch closely!" He aimed his camera. "Act one, scene one of *Clawgantua vs. Gigantopus!* And . . . *action!*" He pressed the remote control at the same time.

KEEE — RUNNNNNNNCH!

The Slither-Matic Deluxe Octo-Prop jerked its tentacles out, ripped the giant back door off the Humongous hangar, and hurled it up in the air.

"Great shot!" Mr. Vickers hooted. Then he frowned. "But . . . wait a minute . . . he's not supposed to do that!"

Everyone watched as the giant door flew up into the clouds and hung there for a moment.

"Wow," gasped Holly, looking straight up.

Then — *whoosh!* — the door dropped right back down to Grover's Mill.

Right back down at Holly.

Sourpuss

WHAM! — the hangar door, now a crumpled, twisted piece of metal, slammed to the ground three inches away from Holly's feet.

"My goodness, that was unexpected!" said Mr. Vickers, smiling as he fumbled with the control box. "I'm sure we can get Gigantopus under control." He pushed the stop button firmly.

Sproing! The box burst apart in his hands.

"Ooops!" Mr. Vickers grinned nervously at the kids. "Everybody in the car!"

But before they could run to safety —

Thhhwupp! Thhhwupp! Two giant tentacles slammed down on the Vickers' old dented station wagon, coiled around it, and hoisted it off the ground.

"Careful, it's a classic!" shouted Mr. Vickers.

CRUNCH! The octopus threw the car down, and the bumpers, doors, and tires blasted off.

"Classic wreck, now!" Mike gasped, diving away as one of the beast's leathery arms snapped like a whip inches from his head.

"Zone alert!" cried Liz. "One out-of-control movie prop, tentacled and dangerous!"

As Mr. Vickers tried desperately to piece the remote back together — *KA-THOONG!* Another long, slithery tentacle slapped down at the top of the Humongous hangar and put a twenty-foot dent in it.

"So maybe it *is* a real octopus?" said Sean.

Two more tentacles snapped swiftly at

the kids. The big suction pads running up and down each arm moved like hundreds of gooey mouths.

"Whatever it is, it's gross!" said Holly.

"And mad!" Liz cried. "And hungry!"

"Run for your lives!" yelled Mike, leaping to safety with Holly and Liz.

Sean made a dash away from the hangar just as one long tentacle slithered out with the oversized fork from the Humongous hit *Attack of the Very Large Kitchen Utensils*.

Gigantopus hurled the big fork at Sean.

THWANG! It missed his head by inches.

"Oooh, bad table manners!" cried Sean.

With another tentacle, Gigantopus shot the large eyeball from *Mysterious Eye Land* at Jeff.

It rolled at him like a supersized bowling ball.

"Help! It's gonna strike!" yelped Jeff.

"Spare him!" cried Liz, who jumped over and pushed Jeff out of the way.

"Everybody this way!" Holly shouted.

"Head for the desert!" She pointed to the wasteland to the west. "He won't follow us. He'll head for town!"

The kids ran full speed across the dusty ground, and tumbled behind a sand dune. Sean climbed up on the dune and looked back at the studio.

"Gigantopus is still attacking," said Sean. The tentacles were snapping at the mountain range from *Snowmonster*.

"There's nowhere to hide around here," said Mike, crouching behind a tiny cactus plant. "Are you guys sure Gigantopus will attack the town?"

Holly shot a look at Sean. Her brother put his hand on Mike's shoulder. "It's the first law of Humongous movies, Mike. Giant Monsters Always Attack Towns."

CRUNCH! The giant octopus hoisted itself across the roof of the hangar.

"Back! Back!" cried Mr. Vickers, still filming as he ran around to the front of the hangar. "Into the background with you!"

"Dad!" yelled Holly from the top of the sand dune. "Get out of there!"

Gigantopus's domed head towered over the hangar, making the building seem like a model.

THWIRP! The eight long tentacles whipped down with incredible speed. They lunged at Mr. Vickers.

"I've got to save Dad!" Holly shrieked, starting back across the sand to the hangar.

Sean grabbed her arm. "No, it's too dangerous! Dad's a Zoner. He'll do okay."

"Keep down," said Liz. "If Gigantopus sees us, he'll come for us, too!"

KEEE — RUNNNNNNNCH! The roof of the studio nearly collapsed under the huge weight.

Just then they saw a low swirl of dust escaping up the road in front of the studio. It was Mr. Vickers, pedaling away on a very small bicycle, his camera still on his shoulder.

"My bike!" called Mike, jumping up and down. "It's way too small for him!"

"Shhhh!" urged Liz, ducking behind the dune.

YEEEOOOWWW! Gigantopus uttered a sudden unearthly roar. He turned. His large red eyes flashed and his suction cups twitched as he spotted the five kids. He snapped his tentacles angrily at them.

"Sorry," said Mike. "I guess I yelled too loud."

WHAM! WHAM! The ground shuddered under Gigantopus's thumping tentacles.

"Maybe now would be a good time for us to escape!" Jeff added quickly.

Mike scrambled across the sand. "Hey, I thought you said he wouldn't come here. The first law of Humongous movies and all that!"

"I guess Gigantopus didn't read the script," said Sean.

The beast, who didn't read the script, suddenly flexed his eight powerful thirty-foot tentacles. He was a blur of oozy suction pads, green leathery skin, and razor-sharp teeth as he slithered across the ground toward the kids.

"The sand!" yelled Jeff. "I can't run that fast!"

Within seconds the beast was there.

"We're octopus food!" cried Mike. "Doomed!"

Then, just as the beast was within striking distance of the five friends, its giant-domed head turned. The creature stopped, twirled its tentacles, and pushed off into the open desert.

"Yahoo!" said Sean. "He's going away! Roll the credits. Turn up the lights. Clear the theater. Shut off the popcorn machine. Get the — "

"Whaaa-ungh!" Holly suddenly went down like a sack of heavy fish.

"Holly?" said Sean. "You don't have to hide. The octopus is gone now."

"I'm not hiding!" she said. "I slipped." She found herself eye level with a pool of shiny stuff. "Whoa, what is this gunk?"

Holly stared at the ground. "That creepy octopus left something slimy!"

Sean stooped. "Gloop," he said helpfully.

"Smells pretty fishy," said Mike, stooping, too.

Holly looked back across the sand. "Yeah, well, whatever it is, Gigantopus is leaving a trail of the fishy gloop. And it starts at the studio."

"Uh-oh!" cried Sean, pointing to a swirl of dust in the desert. "He's turning around again!"

Gigantopus whirled in the sand, his powerful tentacles still dripping gloop, and he headed north.

Toward town.

Toward the center of Grover's Mill!

"Hurry!" yelled Holly. "We have to warn everyone!"

Grabbing a Bite!

When the five friends hit the bottom of Main Street, Grover's Mill was quiet. Very quiet.

Streets were deserted. Cars were abandoned with their engines running. House doors and shop doors were wide open. Bicycles were left on the sidewalk, their wheels spinning slowly.

"Uh-oh, everyone's dead," whispered Mike.

"Mike," said Liz. "Have a little hope, okay?"

Mike was quiet for a second. "Okay, I *hope* everyone's not dead. But I think they are."

Bong! The sound of the Double Dunk Donut Den chimed its hour. The chime echoed eerily up and down the empty streets of Grover's Mill.

Sssss! The oversize pancake clock high atop Usher's House of Pancakes hissed the hour.

"Gigantopus has scared everyone," mumbled Holly as they tiptoed up the wide main road. "What's the deal with this octopus?"

"Well, if this were a movie," said Jeff, "the title would probably tell you what's going on."

"Huh?" said Holly, peering up and down the street for signs of life. Or signs of tentacles.

"You know," Jeff went on. "Like when a movie starts with kids playing around, and it's all jokey and funny, but the title of the movie is *The Giant Squid Beast from Planet Ten*. You just know that a giant squid beast is going to come pretty soon."

Holly looked at Jeff. She wasn't sure if

all that was helpful, but she gave him a smile anyway. "Thanks, Jeff," she said.

Suddenly, out of the distance, came a sound. A motor scooter puttered down the road. In the seat was a very wide, round man. Sitting behind him was another very wide, round man.

"The Double Dunk twins!" shouted Mike.

Yes, and they were singing.

Double Dunk twins is our name,
Twins we are, but not the same.
People love us, that's no shame.
'Cause our donuts bring us fame!

Holly dashed into the street. "Stop! A giant octopus is attacking Grover's Mill!"

Rob Dunk frowned. "We can't stop delivering."

His brother Bob, arms full of brown and white boxes, nodded. "Our donuts must keep rolling!"

Putt-putt! In a second, the twins were gone.

A dusty wind blew up the empty street.

"This is creeping me out," said Liz. "I'm going to go and check my mom's diner. I've got to see if she's okay. Anybody coming with me?"

Mike looked over at Jeff. "Could be our last chance to get some food before the end."

"Egg salad would be cool," said Jeff. He joined Mike and Liz as they headed to Duffey's Diner.

Holly sat down on the sidewalk. "Sean, this is too weird for words. Even for The Weird Zone."

Sean watched their friends go into the diner, come out again, then cross the street to School Road. "Sometimes I think the only way we'll ever get out of here is if Grover's Mill moves."

Holly smiled. "It could be on the other side of the galaxy, and it would still be weird." She looked up at him. "Do you think Gigantopus will be the thing that really gets us?"

"Maybe," said Sean. "But maybe we can stop it. In fact, I think we have to."

Holly knew what he meant. It meant he would do what had to be done. It also meant Sean was scared. Maybe as scared as she was.

"Guys!" Liz came trotting back nearly out of breath. "Everyone is hiding at school. In the secret teachers' shelter deep in the basement."

"Yeah," said Mike, huffing behind her. "Can you believe it?"

Holly shook her head. "So it's just up to us."

Jeff trotted back from across the street. "The Acme truck! It's over there!" He pointed to the Baits Motel's parking lot.

Instantly, something clicked in Holly's brain. "Of course!" she cried. "The lady! She's behind all this. She dropped off the Slither-Matic for Dad. I knew there was something strange about her. If we find her, we find our answers!"

But as Holly ran with her friends up to the front doors of the Baits Motel, she wasn't even sure what questions to ask.

WHAM! The motel doors burst open and a whirl of green suit and red hair leaped out!

"It's her!" cried Holly. "Grab her so she — "

But before Holly could finish, Castor Roddenreel, manager of the motel, came storming out. "Stop that lady!" he called out. "She stayed here, then she ran off with the gill!"

"You mean the bill?" asked Holly.

"No, I mean the *gill*!" the man answered. He pointed to a gaping hole in the top of the motel.

The five kids tore after the lady. Holly was sure that the woman was behind this whole octopus monster attack. They needed to catch her!

"Miss Smith! Miss Jones!" yelled Holly.

"Call off your octopus! He's wrecking our town!"

The lady jerked around at Holly. "AWWK!" she blurted out. Then she leaped into the truck.

"Stop!" Holly started after the woman, but she slipped in another puddle of slime. "Oh, man!" she cried.

Errk — the truck swerved out of the lot and onto Main Street.

"Gigantopus!" cried the lady, pointing up. "Finish what we came here for!"

Holly looked up. A giant eight-pointed shadow passed over the five kids.

THWAM! The huge octopus appeared above them, crashing its tentacles to the ground.

"No!" cried Liz. "We're trapped!"

At just that moment the strains of two voices singing a song came floating around a corner.

"Not the Double Dunk twins!" shrieked Holly.

Yes, the Dunk twins. Gigantopus's red

eyes flashed. It saw the two brothers turning their motor scooter onto Main Street. One tentacle snapped around each of the twins and pulled.

"Don't!" yelled Rob Dunk.

"That's right!" echoed Bob Dunk. "Don't!"

But Gigantopus didn't listen. With a single swift move, his tentacles hurled the twins into a giant mouth, opening on his slimy underside.

One gulp later, the famed donut brothers were no more!

Holly shot up from the ground. "This is not a set, you big monster prop jerk!" she yelled. "It's not pretend! These are our people! This is our town! It's the only home we've got!"

As if to answer her — *KRUNCH!* — Gigantopus twisted the sign off the X-rays Я Us Medical Clinic and threw it to the ground.

Then it coiled up its arms and pushed down.

Gigantopus took off into the desert again.

Liz looked at Holly. "It's doing that weird zigzag thing again! Maybe we should make a move now, before he comes back."

"No!" Holly shook her head. "Second Humongous law. It's — All — Up — To — Us! There's only one place with the right stuff to fight this thing. Only one place equipped to battle giant monsters."

"Battle giant monsters?" Sean looked at her, frowning. Then he slowly started to smile. "Yeah, one place. One *humongous* place!"

"To the studio!" cried Holly. "Now!"

The One Big Thing

Entering the wrecked hangar of Humongous Horror Movie Studios gave Holly the spooks. Gashes in the ceiling let in the sunlight. The huge back door was torn away. There was slime everywhere. Everything was a mess.

"Kind of squishy in here," Liz said.

"And even creepier than before," said Jeff.

But Holly couldn't afford to be scared now. Too much had to be done. She heard the distant sounds of crunching and thumping. Gigantopus was slowly destroying their town. "Everybody spread out! Find something to stop this thing!"

Within minutes, the studio was like a big war room. Everyone was bustling around doing jobs.

Mike pulled the miniature model of Grover's Mill to the center of the floor.

Jeff switched on the radio to WYRD, the Grover's Mill station, where Rock Storm was broadcasting news. "Reports have come in from all over town," he said.

Sean walked around the miniature town and stuck little flags in. "Gigantopus has been sighted here, here, and here!"

Holly stepped over. As she looked down at the table, a sense of terror crept up her spine.

"Connect the dots!" gasped Holly.

"They're little flags," said Jeff.

"Connect the little flags!" Holly cried out. "They're making a shape! An *eight-pointed* shape! An octopus shape!"

"Wow, Holly's right!" Sean added. "And he's leaving slimy gloop wherever he goes. A big octopus-shaped trail of gunk around Grover's Mill."

"What does it all mean?" asked Mike.

"I don't know." Holly scratched her gloopy shirt. "By the way, does anybody else think it's warm in here?"

"It's a little warm but it's way weird," said Liz. "I mean, I know it would be dumb to ask 'Why Grover's Mill?' It's The Zone. So, I guess the question is, how do we stop the big octopus?"

Holly jumped. "Yes! The third law of Humongous Horror Movies! The One Big Thing!"

"The what?" said Mike.

Holly explained. "Every huge, hungry, crazy monster can be defeated by The One Big Thing. It's the one thing that will destroy the monster."

"How about heat?" said Liz. "Intense heat. Your dad used that in a movie once."

"Once!" said Sean, with a chuckle. "More like a hundred times!"

"Right!" said Holly. "Or cold, or lightning, or fire, or water, or . . . water . . ."

"You said water twice," said Mike.

"Water!" Holly blurted out again.

"Three times, now," Mike muttered.

"That's it!" Holly cried. "If the thing really is a giant octopus, it will need water. All we have to do is figure out something with water!"

"Water!" shouted Liz.

Holly frowned. "We got that far, Liz."

"No! I mean, somebody get some water!" cried Liz. "Holly's on fire!"

"What!" Holly turned to see smoke rising from the slime spot on her T-shirt. "Help!"

Jeff dashed to the oversized kitchen set and filled a giant water glass. He splashed it on Holly.

Sssss! Holly's T-shirt hissed and smoked.

But when Jeff threw the water, some of it splashed at Sean. "Hey!" He ducked back. When he did that, he slammed hard right into the fog machine. He pushed down its start button.

POOOOOOOOOOOF!

Within moments, the entire hangar was filled with dense fog.

"Ooops!" said Sean, stumbling around. "How do you turn it off?" He tried to find the switch.

Then — *whoosh!* A soft breeze from the desert pushed the fog out of the room. The air cleared.

And suddenly *she* was there. The green-suited lady with the red hair. Wisps of fog swirled around her as she strode over to the five friends. She stopped at a crater on the Mars set.

"What an entrance!" said Mike. "Just like in the movies. Are you sure you're not an actress?"

"That perfume again," said Jeff. "Wow."

The woman just stood there.

"You!" cried Holly, staring at her. "We almost have no town left because of you and your big dumb octopus monster! Go home!"

The woman stepped over to Holly. She

looked at her with a snarly smile, then ran her fingers through her wavy red hair. "I'm not leaving until I get what I came for."

Holly didn't like the sound of that. "Just who are you? And what are you doing here?"

"Maybe this will explain!" snorted the woman. Slowly she reached her left hand up and gripped something under her chin. And with Holly, Sean, Jeff, Mike, and Liz watching her every move, she began to pull!

Sleeooooop!

The woman tugged a thin layer of spongy stuff off her face. Gooey strings of glue came with it. Then she threw her wig to the floor.

"There's a big green thing under her face!" said Mike, bending to look under.

The big green thing under her face was a big green head! It was a speckly round dome with burning red eyes! Behind the green head were long things twisted up together.

"She's not a regular lady," said Mike.

Liz moved closer to her friends. "And I don't think those are regular braids, either."

Liz was right. The woman shook her dome as if she were tossing her hair loose from a ponytail. Suddenly, eight slithery green tentacles uncoiled and fell over her shoulder. They slapped to the floor behind her.

"Wow!" said Mike. "An octopus lady!"

"Incredible!" gasped Sean. "Dad uses makeup to change regular faces into ugly heads, and — !"

" — And I did the same," the ocotopus lady cut in. "To me, humans are ugly heads. And look at you, no tentacles at all!" She snorted a laugh.

Then the lady spoke again. Only this time her voice was different. It sounded deep and bubbly, as if she were talking underwater. "My name is Octa-Loona! Queen of the Octopus Monsters!"

"Where do you come from, Mars?" asked Jeff.

"Mars!" the green head smirked. "That pitiful planet of surfing zombies? I don't think so. I happen to be Queen of Planet X! And by the way, Mars doesn't have anything like these cardboard craters."

"Thanks for the geography lesson," Holly said. "But I think you'd better go back to Planet X, because we've got lots of other things to — "

"Enough talk!" Octa-Loona interrupted. "It's time for death. Yours!"

The words struck fear in Holly's heart. But her brother stepped over next to her and glared at the octopus woman.

"Sorry, Octa-Looney!" snarled Sean. "We have no time for death. We've got a town to save!"

Octa-Loona's red eyes went wide. Her tentacles twitched. "And how are you going to win? I've got you way outnumbered!"

Then, in a flash . . . flash . . . flash . . .

in eight flashes, actually, Octa-Loona unfurled her tentacles and made a big green fist with each one!

"Anyone for tentacles?" cried the Queen of Planet X.

Within seconds, the fight had begun!

Thonk! Pow! Ka-plang!

"**A**ttack!" shrieked Holly, charging at the eight-tentacled Queen of Planet X.

"Wait! First we need attack props!" cried Sean. He rushed to the castle set from *Dream Dungeon Disco*, and grabbed a shiny sword off the wall.

"Now we attack!" he yelled, charging at Octa-Loona, waving the shiny sword.

Flonk! The sword blade bent in half as he ran. "Uh-oh!" Then the shiny stuff fell off. It was foil.

Sean stopped. "Hey, I thought it was real."

"Ha!" Octa-Loona smirked. "Toys are no

match for me. Here's something real for you!"

THWACK! Sean was hurled back onto the bed of spikes from *Torture, Anyone?* Luckily, the spikes were made of rubber.

"She's winning!" yelled Holly. She dashed across the hangar and came running back with the giant hairy hand from *Pa's Hairy Paws!*

"Oh, want to shake?" Octa-Loona snarled. "Well, okay, let's!"

THWANK! One tentacle snapped around Holly's arms and lifted her into the air. Then it began to shake her up!

"Sto-aaa-ooo-aaa-oop!" moaned Holly as the hairy paw dropped to the floor and a tentacle snapped it away across the room.

"Oh, now you're going to get it!" cried Liz from the kitchen set of *Tiny Folks Fight Big.* She grabbed an enormous pair of scissors.

"Oh, a cutup, are you?" snorted Octa-

Loona. "Didn't anyone tell you that's dangerous?"

"Ha!" Liz snarled back. "I'm just going to even up the sides!" The blades opened as Liz charged.

"Ge-etttt herrrr, Lizzzz!" shouted Holly, still being shaken around above the queen's head.

Holly was amazed at how her friends battled the evil queen. Just like in the movies, they were everywhere, fighting, making incredible moves.

Thwing! Thwong! The octopus queen swung around and faced Liz. A tentacle twirled out and grabbed Liz tightly by her ankles.

"No!" Liz strained as she was hoisted high above the ugly woman.

"Sorry," said Liz, squirming toward Holly. "I tried."

Holly smiled at her. It didn't look good for them, but she knew what she and her friends had to do. Bottom line. Stop Octa-

Loona and her pet. Because if they didn't, the slimy queen would slither off to another town. Gigantopus would wreck it. Then another and another.

Planet after planet! Galaxy after galaxy!

No way! They had to stop this now. Here. On the galactic battlefield known as Grover's Mill!

"Ugh!" grunted Holly, trying to squirm out of the tentacles' grasp. "Got . . . to . . . free . . . ourselves!"

No good. She was caught.

Thwang! Another of Octa-Loona's slithery tentacles grabbed Mike by his foot. "She's got me!" he cried. "It feels creepy on my leg!"

Thwip! Thwap! Sean and Jeff were caught as they tried to pelt her with rubber brains from the set of *Whose Brain Is This, Anyway?*

"Ooooh, yesssss!" the octopus woman wailed. "Puny two-armed humans! I have you all!" Her three remaining tentacles twirled up to her lips. Then she let out a high-pitched whistle. "Eeeeeeeeeeeeeee!"

"Nice sound effects!" said Holly, struggling against the slimy suction pads. "But you can't keep us up here forever!"

"I could!" Octa-Loona blurted out. "But I've got other fish to fry! Get it? And anyway — "

YEEEOOWW! A shocking sound pierced the studio from outside and the front hangar door ripped off its hinges.

Enormous Gigantopus himself crashed inside the studio. His tentacles flailed and slapped!

"My ride is here!" Octa-Loona cried out, clapping with her free tentacles. Then — *thump! thump! thump!* (five *thumps*, actually) she hurled the kids across the room.

Through the open hangar door, Holly saw the destruction Gigantopus had left in Grover's Mill. The water tower was down. The WYRD radio tower was crumpled. Slime was everywhere.

"And now, to finish our plan!" cried Octa-Loona.

"Why do aliens always have to have plans?" snarled Holly. She was feeling very angry.

"Why do humans always need to know?" Octa-Loona snapped back. "Besides, you'll find out when the time is right."

Gigantopus's tentacles wrapped gently around the queen and pulled her to the top of its giant green dome. She sat there.

"To Grover's Mill!" the octopus-headed woman proclaimed. And the beast lumbered off.

Holly turned to her friends. "We can't let this happen! Think of the Dunk twins! Think of Grover's Mill! We need to fight back! We need to stop them! Get the big green octopus and the octo-lady!"

Octa-Loona whirled her dome around and glared with her big red eyes. She pointed her tentacles at Holly. "You want to come so bad? Okay then!"

"B-b-but," sputtered Holly. "What I meant was — "

THWAP! Before Holly could move, the

Gigantopus twirled a tentacle across the floor and grabbed her by the ankle.

"Hey! Not my sister, you don't!" yelled Sean. In a panic, he glanced around. He ran to the set of *Saturn by Saturday* and grabbed a five-foot-long rocket made from wrapping paper tubes.

He charged at top speed, holding the rocket like a spear. "This nose cone is going right for that ugly dome!"

"Sean!" shouted Liz. "Watch out!"

But Octa-Loona saw him, too. "Eat the boy! That'll teach him to call me ugly!"

Suddenly, Gigantopus dropped Holly — *thud!* — and flung his tentacles out for Sean.

THWONG! Sean's rocket spear flew apart in his hands. "Oh, not again!"

Gigantopus's powerful suction pads grasped Sean and pulled him toward the big dome.

"No — " Holly began to scream, jumping up from the floor. "You leave him alone!"

Suddenly — *SLOOOOOP!*

Sean was slurped up into the giant mouth in the octopus's dome!

"Sean?" Holly cried out. "Sean! Answer me!"

But the only answer Holly got was — *BWAP!* — as the giant octopus burped.

Alone — With Them!

"**S**ean is my brother! I gotta go!" Holly screamed as the last of Sean vanished into the beast's slimy mouth.

"Go where?" asked Liz. "You don't mean — "

But without another word, Holly raced across the hangar, and leaped into the slimy jaws of the giant octopus!

"Yuuuuuuuuuck!" she screamed.

When Holly jumped she expected to land in a soft oozy mushy octopus mouth with lots of slimy saliva dripping all over her. And maybe teeth.

CLONG! Something closed shut behind her.

Octopus jaws?

No, Holly skidded across a floor. A metal floor. In a metal room. And in a dim light shining down from the ceiling of the room, she saw her brother Sean sprawled on the floor next to her, totally slimed.

"Sean! You're alive!" she cried.

"Yeah," he mumbled. "But I feel all gross."

Next to him, hunched on the floor, were two very identical, very wide, very round men.

"And the Double Dunk twins!" cried Holly. "You're alive, too!"

"And getting thinner by the minute," Rob Dunk complained. "I'm sure our Double Dunk clock has struck noon by now!"

"But no one has fed us yet," agreed his brother Bob. "What kind of place is this?"

"It's a giant octopus," said Holly. "I think."

"Well," said Rob. "Did you come to save us?"

Holly got up from the floor. "I think it's a little too soon to say." She looked around. The "mouth" that had eaten them was really a hatch in the middle of the floor. And above them, in the center of the ceiling, was another hatch of some kind, with a window in the middle.

Sean shook his head. "I think we got ourselves into a really big mess this time, Holly. Sorry I got swallowed. You didn't really have to come after me."

"Oh, hey, it was something to do." Holly smiled. She tried to peer up through the hatch. "We have to see what's up there."

"Perhaps we can be of help?" said Rob Dunk. "You may not have noticed, but my brother and I are big, like our donuts. Why not stand on us?"

Rob Dunk and Bob Dunk rolled to the middle of the room, right under the top hatch. Holly and Sean stepped carefully up onto their stomachs and peered through the window.

"Whoa!" gasped Holly when she stepped down again. "Now we've really done it. Weird is weird, Sean, but this is an actual alien spaceship! And we're inside it!"

"So it's definitely *not* a real octopus," said Sean.

"There's a latch up there," said Holly. "If we can turn the handle, we can open it. Then we jump in behind that big control panel. Let's go."

The two kids stepped up on the twins' round stomachs again and quietly turned the hatch handle.

"This is it, Holly," said Sean, placing his feet squarely on Rob Dunk's waist. "With just a little bounce, we can be up there. Ready?"

"Ready," said Holly, holding her breath.

Rob Dunk turned to his brother and rubbed his middle. "The things we do!"

"Yes, the things!" agreed his twin.

Boing! Boing! Boing! Sean and Holly bounced once, twice, three times, and they were in the air! In a flash, the kids were through the hatch and into the upper control room.

They dived behind a large control panel, lighted with strangely colored lights.

"Good," whispered Sean. "No one saw us."

Holly nodded, looking around. They were inside an octopus-shaped spaceship, in a large eight-sided room with a domed ceiling. Running around the walls was a long control panel. Seated at the controls were creatures with green domes like Octa-Loona.

Two of the octopuses wore dusty overalls.

"Hey," whispered Holly. "It's the two Acme delivery guys. Only, now they have octopus heads!"

"On them it looks good," Sean whispered.

Whrr! Bzzzz! Nnnnn! The equipment buzzed.

"Check the Octo Meter!" commanded a watery voice from somewhere in the cen-

ter of the room. "The Octo Scope reports that we are ready to begin the Octo Plan!"

Holly peered up. She saw *her*.

Octa-Loona, Queen of Planet X, her tentacles twitching down over the arms of a throne. The throne was made in the shape of a big seashell.

The queen rose. "My people, we are so close to fulfilling our mission. This is a perfect occasion for the singing of our planetary anthem!"

She strode to the center of the control room. Her voice got all underwatery as she began to sing her patriotic alien song. It went like this.

> *Oh, splendid Planet X!*
>   *Our tentacles we flex!*
> *We bow our domey necks*
>   *to you,*
> *We make our starry treks*
>   *for you,*
> *Oh, Planet, Planet X!*

While Octa-Loona was singing her song, the workers at the controls turned and faced her.

Slimy tears dribbled down their domes.

They began to sniffle. The song makes them homesick," whispered Holly.

"Yeah, well, it makes me just regular sick," Sean grumbled. The octopus monsters wiped their tears then placed their tentacles over their hearts.

This caused Gigantopus to slow down. Suddenly Sean lost his balance. He fell back into Holly and they both sprawled out onto the floor.

"Ooops!" mumbled Sean.

"Ah!" said Octa-Loona, whirling around. "Our human specimens!"

The two octo-monsters with overalls came over. Their tentacles shot straight out, trapping Holly and Sean in a cage of slimy arms.

Octa-Loona strode over. "Our people will enjoy these two when we make our triumphant return."

"Return?" Holly swallowed hard. "To where?"

"Didn't you hear the song?" Octa-Loona said with a smile. "To splendid Planet X, of course!"

An Octopus With a View

"Planet X?" asked Holly. She turned to Sean. "What? How? When?"

But Octa-Loona didn't bother to explain. She simply snapped her tentacles. "Press the Octo Pedal!" she boomed. "Start the Octo Rockets!"

The craft began to whir. Holly could feel the octopus-shaped spaceship tilting suddenly. Then it began to lift up into the air. Her legs felt tingly, as if she were going up in an elevator.

"Sean, we're moving!" cried Holly. She turned to the queen. "Okay, what is the Octo Plan?" she demanded.

"Ah, the Octo Plan!" The leathery mouth

on Octa-Loona's dome stretched into a smile. "Wasn't it clever how we delivered our attack ship to your father?"

"Yeah," said the chubby Acme guy. "They thought we were humans! Dat's a good one!"

Octa-Loona folded her tentacles. "The Octo Plan is no secret. All you have to do is read." She pointed at a giant blackboard on the wall.

"Let me guess," said Holly. "The Octo List?"

There were four items listed.

1. Lock up Octo House.
2. Blast off for Earth.
3. Locate typical Earth town.
4. Bring back sample.

"So what are we?" asked Sean. "Samples?"

"No," said Octa-Loona. "That is!" She pointed to the Octo Screen on the control panel. In view on the screen was the entire town of Grover's Mill below them.

Holly saw from the view screen that the

ship was rising slowly over the town. The shiny trail of slime on the ground below was steaming and smoking in the hot sun. It formed a huge octopus-shaped star completely around Grover's Mill.

Holly gasped and looked at Sean. "That's it! The slime," she started. "The trail of slime."

Sean waited. "I don't get it."

Holly gulped. She knew it was triple weird, but every one of her brain cells told her it was true. The octo-creatures from Planet X were going to *take* Grover's Mill!

"Don't you see?" Holly said. "It all makes sense! Just like when my T-shirt started burning. The slime is burning into the earth around Grover's Mill! It's separating the town from the ground around it! These creatures are going to rip Grover's Mill right out of the ground and take it with them! Back to Planet X!"

"Whoa!" Sean frowned. "That sounds just a little weird."

"I know!" cried Holly. "It's a lot weird!"

Octa-Loona stepped over to the two kids. Her tentacles slithered back over her shoulders and braided themselves quietly. "Your sister is right. We're taking Grover's Mill back to Planet X!"

Sean turned to Octa-Loona. "Bring a whole town across the galaxy? How?"

"We have the technology!" Octa-Loona declared. "Just watch!"

The kids watched, but what they saw was unbelievable!

As the craft whirred high over Grover's Mill, the eight giant tentacles stiffened straight out. Then from the ends of the tentacles shot thick cables that extended hundreds of feet down to the ground.

Suddenly — *flang! flang! flang!* (eight *flangs*, actually) — the ends of the cables plugged into the points of the octopus-shaped star that the slime had made around Grover's Mill. The star that Gigantopus had made.

The cables began to turn. They hummed. They groaned. They drilled *under* Grover's Mill.

"All secure, your majesty!" said the overall-wearing, pencil-chewing octopus delivery guy.

VRRRRRR! The spaceship began to lift.

And as it lifted, the tentacles strained and the cables pulled at the ground. Harder, harder.

"The earth's crust around your town has been burned through," explained Octa-Loona, beaming at how the Octo Plan was working. "Now, a simple tug . . . and . . ."

KKKKKKKKKKRRRRRIPPPPPP!

In a single, swift move, with an awful ripping sound that made Holly feel sick, Grover's Mill, the entire town, *peeled* off from the ground beneath it!

The eight powerful tentacles pulled up, the spaceship lifted, and Grover's Mill dangled above the ground. Dirt and roots and sewer pipes tumbled back down into the vast hole the town left behind.

Grover's Mill swung back and forth slowly on the cables.

"This is so unbelievable!" shrieked Holly.

Sean nodded, his eyes wide in shock.

"Unbelievable, perhaps," said Octa-Loona, daubing red lipstick on her green leathery lips. "Like your father's movies?"

The Queen of Planet X laughed as the giant ship continued to rise.

Typical? As If!

RMMMM! Gigantopus's engines rumbled louder and louder. Holly knew time was running out. Soon, the ship would blast off to Planet X with Grover's Mill hanging underneath it.

Who knows what would happen to Grover's Mill out there. The whole town could just slide off into space!

All her friends — Liz, Mike, Jeff — were down there. Her parents. Her life. Her room.

All of a sudden Sean started laughing.

"What!" screeched Octa-Loona, her red eyes squinting and glaring at him.

"Typical?" Sean roared out. He pointed

to the Octo List. "I just got that! Grover's Mill — typical? I don't think so!"

Holly instantly knew what he was doing. She started to laugh, too. "Oh, yeah, that *is* funny! You'd be much better off taking Washington or New York or Hollywood."

"Grover's Mill is the absolute *weirdest* town in the galaxy!" Sean added.

Holly nodded sincerely. "Really, it's for your own good, Ms. Loona. No way do you want us!"

"Why not just put it back?" said Sean. "We'll go home and you'll go home and everybody will just forget the whole thing."

"Ha!" cried Octa-Loona. "If this town were really as strange as you say, there would be a book about it! No, there would be a whole bunch of books about it!"

Sean looked at Holly. Holly looked at Sean.

"It's too late anyway!" Octa-Loona declared, smiling a nasty smile. She thumped over to the octopus looking at the screen. "Nothing can stop us now."

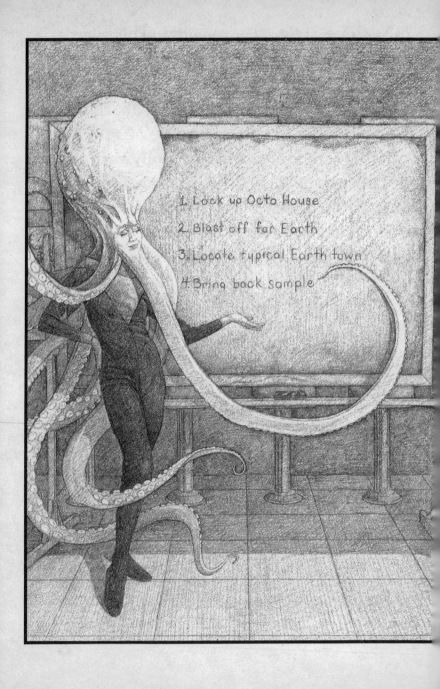

1. Lock up Octo House

2. Blast off for Earth

3. Locate typical Earth town

4. Bring back sample

Nothing can stop us now. The words burned themselves into Holly's brain. Nothing. *No thing*. She thought again of her father's list of things. The third Humongous law.

Heat. Cold. Fire. Water. Water?

As the ship began to move, and Grover's Mill swung back and forth, something large and round and blue came into view on the screen.

"Lake Lake," Holly whispered. "Of course!" She turned to Sean and leaned closer so that the Acme guys couldn't hear. "Gigantopus is only a spaceship, but Looney and her Loonettes are real octopeople. They need water. Remember how she was so excited about fish and stuff?"

Sean nodded. "You're right. Water! We have to make them go back down. It's our only chance . . ."

"Besides," whispered Holly, "if I know Dad, he's going to shoot his movie even if the town gets kidnapped to another galaxy.

You know, keep those cameras rolling?"

"Just the sort of final Humongous scene his movie's going to need," said Sean. "It's perfect."

"Hey!" shouted the chubby Acme guy. "What are you two whispering about?" His green dome was twitching to hear.

"Just talking about one of the nice things about Grover's Mill," Holly said more loudly. "For one thing, I mean, a lot of people come here for the water."

"Water?" said the chubby Acme guy. His dome mouth fell open. It was dry.

Octa-Loona turned to Holly. A tentacle curled up to her face and rubbed her leathery lips.

"Now, Holly," said Sean, turning to her. "Why do you think they call it Lake Lake?"

"Because it has so much water in it!" she said.

"Correct!" said Sean. "Boy, just the word *water* makes me thirsty. Aren't you thirsty, Holly?"

Eeek! Eeek! Grover's Mill swung back and forth on the cables.

"Very thirsty," Holly said.

"I sure am thirsty, too," Sean went on. "Gosh, I'd give anything for just a sip of that great Lake Lake water. It sure would quench my thirst. I wouldn't be so thirsty. Thirsty, thirsty, thirsty."

"Thirsty, thirsty, thirsty," said Holly, watching on the Octo Screen as Grover's Mill swung back and forth on the long wires, a gaping octopus-shaped hole in the ground below it. "Thirsty, thirs — "

"ENOUGH!" screamed Octa-Loona.

One by one, all the octo-creatures turned their domed heads to the queen. Their big red eyes were all sad. Their green lips were dry.

"Oh, okay!" cried Octa-Loona finally. She pushed some buttons on the control panel. "I'm putting the town down for a minute. One minute, that's all! Then we go!"

RRRR! The giant ship descended.

THUD! Grover's Mill was dropped back into place. The cables went slack and the ship hovered over the watery blue water of Lake Lake.

"Hurray!" shouted the octo-creatures. They clapped their tentacles and began to sing again.

> *Queen Octa-Loona!*
> *She's not a tuna!*
> *She's an octopus,*
> *And she looks out for us,*
> *'Cause she's our queen!*

In that instant of octopus joy, the two Acme guys loosened their hold on the two kids. It was then that Holly and Sean decided to make their move.

In a flash, the two kids dropped back down through the hatch to the mouth room.

"Hey!" yelled the chubby Acme guy. "The two kids — they're gettin' away!"

Too late! Holly jammed the hatch shut, then turned to Rob and Bob Dunk. "Hurry, we're getting out of here!"

"Oh, have we landed?" asked Rob Dunk.

Holly looked at Sean, "Uh, not quite. But, um, can you swim?"

Rob looked at his brother. "We can float!"

"Yes, float," said Bob.

"That's good enough!" said Sean. "Let's go!"

Holly opened the bottom hatch. Wind blew in from the outside. Lake Lake was rippling calmly right below them. It was like watching a movie.

"This is so weird," she said, turning to Sean. "I mean, can we actually do this?"

Woop-woop! An alarm sounded.

"I don't think we have a choice," said Sean.

"They're escaping!" shouted Octa-Loona. "Close the hatch!"

VRRRT! The mouth hatch began to close! The opening was getting smaller and smaller. Soon the two kids and the two twins would be trapped forever. They had to act swiftly!

Rob and Bob Dunk sat down next to the open hatch. Holly and Sean climbed on their backs.

"Here we go!" cried Holly. With one push, she and Sean pushed the twins out of the hatch.

"Agggghhh!" shrieked Rob Dunk.

"Ooooggghhh!" shrieked Bob Dunk.

The two kids held on to the two heavy men and fell like, well, like two kids holding on to two heavy men!

They fell fast, very fast.

Straight for Lake Lake.

10

Splash of the Titans!

Lake Lake.

A giant O of water sitting there like warm milk in the bottom of a cereal bowl. Only bluer.

To Holly it seemed as if the lake were rushing up at them at incredible speed.

"It's going to be a short flight!" cried Sean.

"We're gonna dunk!" screamed Holly.

"Our specialty!" yelled Rob and Bob.

SPLASH! They slammed into the water hard.

SPLOING! They bobbed back to the surface with incredible force. The waves they

made drove the two kids and the Dunk twins right to shore.

Holly and Sean jumped off and sputtered up onto the beach at the foot of the Grover's Mill beach clubhouse.

"We made it!" yelled Sean. "I can't believe we're actually back home!"

"But home may be moving to another galaxy unless we hurry!" cried Holly.

Rob and Bob Dunk hustled to their feet and began to run. Rob turned to Bob and said, "Are you thinking what I'm thinking?"

"Yes!" cried Bob. "Octopus-shaped donuts!"

WOOOOM! The giant octopus-shaped spaceship was hovering over the lake and lowering a giant straw into the water.

"This is too weird for words!" gasped Holly. She scrambled up the beach toward town. "You know what we have to do, Sean. Come on!"

But even as she said that, Holly knew it was next to impossible to stop Octa-

Loona. Everyone was probably still hiding underground in the school. Liz, Mike, and Jeff were who knows where. And her father . . .

This was one movie that didn't look like it would have a happy ending.

Then, suddenly — *Rrrr! Errch! Eeeeek! Rmmm!*

And, just like in the movies, they were all there.

Liz, Mike, and Jeff were there, exactly where they needed to be. Riding in the Acme delivery truck, with a big covered shape on the back. It was being driven by none other than the moviemaker himself, Todd Vickers!

"Our friends!" yelped Sean.

"Woo-hoo!" shouted Jeff, jumping from the truck as it screeched to a stop on the beach.

"You guys are excellent!" cried Mike. "You're saving our town!"

"Yessss!" Liz hissed, smiling big at her

best friend, and giving Holly a double high five.

"We have no time to waste!" cried Mr. Vickers. "This lighting is perfect for the final battle scene. Let's get to work!"

Holly glanced over at Sean and shook her head, smiling. That's our dad, she thought.

Within minutes, the five kids had helped Mr. Vickers unload the giant shape from the truck and down to the water.

Mr. Vickers suddenly pulled the canvas off the shape. "Behold! Clawgantua, the Clawed Avenger!"

VRRR! The giant octopus-shaped spacecraft was pulling away from Lake Lake.

"Oh, no!" shouted Liz. "They're leaving!"

"That's not the way it goes!" Mr. Vickers said. "We're doing the final battle between Clawgantua and Gigantopus!" He fiddled furiously with the claw controls inside the giant crablike monster. "Oh, I've waited a long time for this moment!"

"Hurry!" said Holly. "They're getting away!"

Mr. Vickers stepped back. "It's ready!"

Holly and Sean climbed into the mechanical body of the giant double-clawed creature and plunked down on kitchen chairs inside. All around them were dozens of electric controls.

Mike, Liz, and Jeff jumped in next to them.

"I hope this stuff works," said Holly.

"Me, too," said Liz. "Our town's at stake."

Mr. Vickers tapped the side of the lumpy prop. "Cameras are rolling! And . . . action!"

"Attack!" screamed Holly and Sean together, as they hit the start switch on the giant-clawed monster.

It was incredible. The scaly, big-clawed monster shot off the beach and into the water. In an instant it was roaring across the lake.

"Go, Claw, go!" cried Mike. "It's snack time!"

The giant spiny shell sliced through the calm water just as Gigantopus began to rise.

Jeff hit the lever that said PINCH.

PINCH! Clawgantua went right for one of Gigantopus's tentacles and pinched the end!

"Yes!" cheered Sean, wheeling the big crab around for another charge. "Score one for the Clawed Avenger!"

Woooo-woooo! The octopus ship sounded its alarm. With one damaged tentacle, it leaned over toward the water. Sean steered the giant crab for another tentacle. Then another and another.

"Yessss!" cried Holly, controlling the claws.

PINCH! PINCH! (Eight pinches, actually) and within moments Mr. Vickers's sea prop had snapped and clawed the ends off of all the cables connecting Grover's Mill to the octo-ship.

Shaking and wobbly, Gigantopus rose slowly over the lake. It was defeated!

"We did it!" Holly cried out, as she and Sean, Liz, Mike, and Jeff drove Clawgantua up onto the beach. They climbed out and cheered.

Suddenly — *VOOOOM!* Gigantopus's giant rocket engines howled and rumbled.

Then it dived full speed — right at the kids!

It's a Weird World After All

The giant eight-pointed shape filled the sky!

"It's coming for us!" cried Holly, racing across the sand. "To the clubhouse, hurry!"

Then — *Errrrk!* Gigantopus stopped just above the beach. It hovered there. Holly looked up to the mouth hatch under the ship. She saw *her*.

"It's Octa-Loona!" said Sean. "She's mad!"

The Queen of Planet X was shaking her eight tentacles at Holly and her friends! "I'll be back!" she sputtered. "I'll get your town some day!"

"Excellent!" exclaimed Mr. Vickers, his

movie camera still on his shoulder. "The fifth Humongous law! Always Leave Room for a Sequel!"

An instant later, the eight-pointed octopus ship sped away into the sky and disappeared.

"Back to your own galaxy!" yelled Mike.

"Or, maybe," said Sean, looking over at Holly, "to one of those really typical towns?"

Holly wondered about that. "Oh, well. I guess we'll read about it someday."

"Perfect final shot!" shouted Mr. Vickers, his camera still focused on the sky where the ship vanished. "Couldn't be better! The spacecraft leaving. They might be back, we don't know. The octopus lady vowing revenge. It's perfect!"

Holly looked over at Sean and smiled. She turned to her father. "As long as you're happy, Dad."

Mr. Vickers was happy later that night, too. Back at Humongous Studios he showed the kids everything he had filmed that day. After it was done, he said, "Wasn't that brilliant? It nearly moves me to tears. I have no doubt that soon the telephone will begin ringing with offers from Hollywood!"

Mr. Vickers stared at the phone.

He stared some more.

He sat down next to it and stared some more. He picked it up, listened, then put it down again.

"Dad?" said Holly.

"Shhh!" Mr. Vickers held up his hand.

Brrrrrrrrrrrng!

Mr. Vickers leaped for the phone. "Yes, yes. Certainly. Uh-huh. Yes. Tomorrow is perfect! Yes!" He put the phone down. "Ah!"

"What is it, Dad?" asked Sean. "Next stop, Hollywood?"

"Not exactly," said Mr. Vickers. "I just ordered a giant mechanical spider with fangs and — "

WHAM! The hangar door slammed and the five friends tore off toward Grover's Mill.

Jeff turned to his friends. "You know the best part? Mr. Vickers said we could take out the Clawed Avenger whenever we want!"

"I wonder if it would fit in Beach Pool," said Liz with a grin. "We could really have fun with it."

Mike had a thoughtful look. "Who do you think would win in a fight? Clawgantua or the Baits Motel?"

Bong! The Double Dunk donut clock chimed.

Sssss! The Usher pancake pan hissed the hour.

Holly looked out over the town, already starting to rebuild.

Grover's Mill.

Otherwise known as The Weird Zone.